HOPSCOTCH
TWISTY TALES

The
Three Little Pigs
and the
New Neighbour

by Andy Blackford and Tomislav Zlatic

This story is based on the traditional fairy tale,
The Three Little Pigs, but with a new twist.
You can read the original story in
Hopscotch Fairy Tales. Can you
make up your own twisty tale?

First published in 2010 by
Franklin Watts
338 Euston Road
London
NW1 3BH

Franklin Watts Australia
Level 17/207 Kent Street
Sydney
NSW 2000

Text © Andy Blackford 2010
Illustrations © Tomislav Zlatic 2010

A CIP catalogue record for this book is available
from the British Library.

ISBN 978 1 4451 0175 0 (hbk)
ISBN 978 1 4451 0181 1 (pbk)

Series Editor: Melanie Palmer
Series Advisor: Catherine Glavina
Series Designer: Peter Scoulding

Printed in China

Franklin Watts is a division of
Hachette Children's Books,
an Hachette UK company
www.hachette.co.uk

Once there were three little pigs.
One lived in a house made of straw,
one lived in a house made of sticks,
and one in a house made of bricks.

One day, a new neighbour moved in next door to the straw house. "Oh no!" cried the little pig. "It's the Big Bad Wolf!"

5

All day the wolf worked hard, sorting out his new home. "Now I'm hungry," he said, and prepared himself a tasty dinner.

But he knocked over the pepper pot. The pepper went everywhere!

Wolf coughed and sneezed and choked on all the pepper. It even got in his eyes.

"I need water," he gasped, "but I haven't got any! Perhaps that little pig next door will help me."

9

The wolf knocked on the
first little pig's door.

The pig was so scared,
he squealed, "Go away!
There's nobody at home!"

The wolf knocked harder. But the door was only made of straw, so his paw went straight through.

The little pig ran to his brother's house made of sticks.

"Help! Let me in! The Big Bad Wolf is after me!" he squealed.

"Oh no!" wheezed the wolf,
"There's no one at home.
I'll try next door. The little
pig there might help me."

15

The wolf knocked on the door and the two little pigs quickly hid.

"Let me in!" the wolf spluttered.
But no one answered. "Maybe
there's someone upstairs," he
thought and went to climb up.

STICK TOWER

But the wolf was heavy and the house was only made of sticks. The roof broke and he fell right through!

"Oh dear! What a mess!"
the wolf groaned.
"Perhaps the little pig
next door will help me."

The two little pigs ran next door
to their brother's house.
"Help!" they cried. "The Big
Bad Wolf is trying to eat us up!"

25

As the wolf knocked on the door, the third little pig shouted: "Go away! My house is made of bricks! You'll never get in and eat us up!"

"But I don't want to eat you up!
I only want some water!" coughed
the wolf.

The three little pigs laughed. Then they gave the wolf as much water as he could drink, and plenty more!

Put these pictures in the correct order.
Which event do you think is most important?
Now try to make up a different ending!

Puzzle 2

1. I'm very hungry.

2. Here is what the wolf needs.

3. I need to escape!

4. I must find some water.

5. I'm scared of being eaten!

6. It's hard work moving house.

Choose the correct speech bubbles for each character. Can you think of any others? Turn over to find the answers.

Answers

Puzzle 1

The correct order is: 1e, 2a, 3d, 4c, 5f, 6b

Puzzle 2

The big bad wolf: 1, 4, 6

The three little pigs: 2, 3, 5

Look out for more Hopscotch Twisty Tales and Fairy Tales:

TWISTY TALES

The Three Little Pigs and the New Neighbour
ISBN 978 1 4451 0175 0*
ISBN 978 1 4451 0181 1

Jack and the Bean Pie
ISBN 978 1 4451 0176 7*
ISBN 978 1 4451 0182 8

Brownilocks and the Three Bowls of Cornflakes
ISBN 978 1 4451 0177 4 *
ISBN 978 1 4451 0183 5

Cinderella's Big Foot
ISBN 978 1 4451 0178 1*
ISBN 978 1 4451 0184 2

Little Bad Riding Hood
ISBN 978 1 4451 0179 8*
ISBN 978 1 4451 0185 9

Sleeping Beauty – 100 Years Later
ISBN 978 1 4451 0180 4*
ISBN 978 1 4451 0186 6

FAIRY TALES

The Three Little Pigs
ISBN 978 0 7496 7905 7

Little Red Riding Hood
ISBN 978 0 7496 7901 9*
ISBN 978 0 7496 7907 1

Goldilocks and the Three Bears
ISBN 978 0 7496 7903 3

Hansel and Gretel
ISBN 978 0 7496 7904 0

Rapunzel
ISBN 978 0 7496 7900 2*
ISBN 978 0 7496 7906 4

Rumpelstiltskin
ISBN 978 0 7496 7902 6*
ISBN 978 0 7496 7908 8

The Elves and the Shoemaker
ISBN 978 0 7496 8543 0

The Ugly Duckling
ISBN 978 0 7496 8538 6*
ISBN 978 0 7496 8544 7

Sleeping Beauty
ISBN 978 0 7496 8545 4

The Frog Prince
ISBN 978 0 7496 8540 9 *
ISBN 978 0 7496 8546 1

The Princess and the Pea
ISBN 978 0 7496 8541 6*
ISBN 978 0 7496 8547 8

Dick Whittington
ISBN 978 0 7496 8542 3 *
ISBN 978 0 7496 8548 5

Cinderella
ISBN 978 0 7496 7417 5

Snow White and the Seven Dwarfs
ISBN 978 0 7496 7418 2

The Pied Piper of Hamelin
ISBN 978 0 7496 7419 9

Jack and the Beanstalk
ISBN 978 0 7496 7422 9

The Three Billy Goats Gruff
ISBN 978 0 7496 7420 5

The Emperor's New Clothes
ISBN 978 0 7496 7421 2